D1474561

RONI SCHOTTER

EFAN
THE GREAT

Illustrated by Rodney Pate

Lothrop, Lee & Shepard Books
New York

For Jesse

Text copyright © 1986 by Roni Schotter.
Illustrations copyright © 1986 by Rodney Pate.

Printed in the United States of America.
First Edition

1 2 3 4 5 6 7 8 9 10

Library of Congress Cataloging in Publication Data
Schotter, Roni.   Efan the great.
Summary: A young boy finds a way to give his family the Christmas tree they can't afford. 1. Children's stories, American. [1. Christmas—Fiction. 2. Afro-Americans—Fiction. 3. City and town life—Fiction] I. Pate, Rodney, ill.   II. Title. PZ7.S3765Ef 1986   [Fic]   84-25070
ISBN 0-688-04986-9
ISBN 0-688-04987-7 (lib. bdg.)

It was the morning of the day before the night before Christmas. Efan Little was ten years old, and in all his life he had never had a Christmas tree. In fact, this year, things were so bad on 128th Street that not even Old Woman had a tree. And she loved Christmas better than anyone in the world.

But Efan Little had a plan. Tomorrow, when his mother and sister woke up on Christmas morning, they were going to find a real, live Christmas tree standing in the parlor staring at them. And tomorrow, when Old Woman was missing Christmas more than anyone in the world, Efan was going to invite her in and show her the tree.

Efan reached his arms over his head and stretched the sleep from his body. He threw on his clothes and slipped out of his room into the cold air of the bathroom. He felt happy and full of Christmas, and so he sang a Christmas song.

"Hmmm muh muh
Brush those teeth
I ain't singin'
About a Christmas wreath.

"Hmmm muh muh
Do wah wah dee
I'm gonna get us
A Christmas tree.

"Hmmm muh muh
Brush those teeth
I ain't singin'
About . . ."

"Efan," his mother called to him. "Are you making that racket?"

Efan opened the door. His mother stood in front of him, dressed and ready for work. In the light of the bathroom, her face was the color of warm apple butter.

"Mama," Efan shouted, grabbing on to her neck. "I'm singing my Christmas song. Tomorrow is a special day."

"I know, Efan." His mother smiled. "But you'd better sing a little softer, or you'll wake your big sister. And you know what she's like when she's mad!"

"Too late!" Efan yelled, ducking. WOMP. A pillow hit him square in the face.

"Who do you think you are, sounding off like some

4

old wino when I'm trying to get my rest?" Efan's sister's voice was thick with sleep. Her face was puffed and swollen like a pie fresh from the oven.

"I ain't no wino, Mean Margaret. When you don't get your beauty rest, you meaner than a donkey and twice as ugly."

"You calling me donkey?" Margaret picked up her pillow again. "You asking for it."

"You're both donkeys." Their mother laughed and grabbed Margaret's pillow away. She reached for the door. "The market's open tonight for Christmas Eve, so I have to work late. There's lunch and dinner in the icebox. Take care of each other, and try not to fight."

"We won't fight," Margaret said. "Because I'm going back to bed. Don't you dare wake me up, Efan Ugly."

"I may be ugly, but I ain't crazy," Efan said, bowing to her as if she was a princess.

Two doors slammed closed. Efan's mother and Margaret were gone. Efan was alone. It was eight-fifteen, and the whole day lay ahead of him like a huge uneaten cake.

Efan tiptoed into his room. Under his mattress, in a brown envelope, was his life's savings: six dollars and sixty-three cents. He tucked the envelope deep into his back pocket and smiled. He grabbed his jacket, his mittens, and his hat and wrote a quick note to Margaret.

> Dear Kind Miss Margaret,
>   I've gone to bring back Christmas.
>   Signed,
>   Your brother,
>   Efan the Good

6

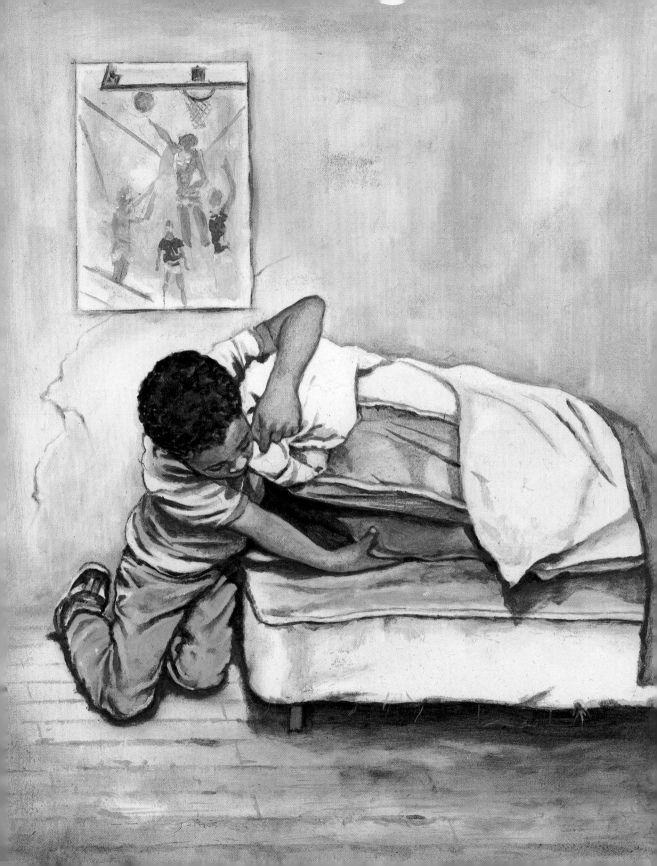

Outside, the world was cold and raw and the color of old newspapers. Efan hunched into his jacket and pulled his collar up around his neck.

One Hundred Twenty-eighth Street was a dead end. Right smack across it was the cement wall of the highway, where everyone piled their trash at the end of each day. Once in a while, a garbage truck rumbled up like a huge, groaning monster. In a few noisy gulps, it swallowed all the garbage. Then, for a few days, 128th Street was clean. But it had been more than a week since the truck had come, and now magazines and newspapers circled and dove in the air like crazy airplanes. Beer cans and broken bottles rolled back and forth against the wall, and skinny no-color cats sniffed the trash cans, hunting for something to eat.

"Efan Little. What are you doing this mean gray morning?" a deep voice called down from above Efan's head.

Efan looked up. There was Old Woman in her bathrobe. She was setting out bowls and cups along the edge of her fire escape.

"It's a secret," Efan said, touching his back pocket and feeling important. "What are you doing? It's way too cold for a picnic."

Old Woman laughed her big laugh that sounded like a song. "This ain't for me, Efan Silly. It's for the pigeons and sparrows. Tomorrow is Christmas, you know. We human folk may be wanting and needing, but my birds are gonna feast."

"Hey there, Efan!" Mrs. Gadsden yelled to them. "How are you, Old Woman?" Mrs. Gadsden cooked breakfast at the Jubilee Star Diner where they served "Only the Finest." She wore a special chef's hat and she always smelled of fresh-brewed coffee and morning toast.

"Morning, Efan Little," Mr. Slater called from up the block. He was wearing his old uniform and his engineer's cap.

"Morning, Caboose," Efan shouted. Mr. Slater's real name was James, but everyone called him Caboose. Long ago, before Efan was born, Caboose used to drive huge freight trains halfway across the country and then bring them home again.

Up the street, Efan could hear singing. His feet moved along the pavement in time to the music. It was the High Tones. They didn't go to school, and they didn't go to work. Rain or shine, snow or blow, they were out on the street or in somebody's lobby doing what they called harmo-nizing.

Efan stopped for a moment to enjoy the sweet sound, but then someone called out to him from the corner.

"Eeeefan Lit-tle." The voice sounded heavy and slow like someone who was half-asleep. "Want to make some extra bread?"

There, wearing a fancy gray hat, was Spider Stokes, the meanest dude on 128th Street. Spider never did a day's work, but somehow he always seemed to have enough to get by with. He even had a whole staff of people to run errands for him. Efan's friend Angel was one of them. Angel would go to 125th Street carrying a small bag of stuff hidden under his coat. When he came back a few hours later, the stuff would be gone, and in its place would be a pile of money. Angel always gave all the money to Spider, who paid him a dollar. Once, Efan had

asked Angel why he didn't just keep all that money instead of giving it to Spider. But Angel had just looked at Efan as if he was crazy.

"How 'bout it, my man?" Spider crooked one of his thin black fingers and beckoned. His eyes and nose and mouth moved to the center of his face as if someone was pinching them. His long legs jerked left and then right.

Efan thought about the money in his back pocket. It would be pretty good to make another dollar. That way, he could get an extra big tree. But there was something about Spider that always made Efan feel sick. Like he'd just swallowed a bucket of raw eggs. "No, thanks," he said. Spider started to say something, but Efan didn't wait to hear it. He just took off as fast as he could. He ran and ran, until 128th Street was far behind him.

He didn't stop running until he was across the street from Jimmy's Great Day Snack Store and Emporium. The lot next door to Jimmy's was usually gray and covered with garbage, but overnight a forest of fir trees had sprouted, and with it, hundreds of customers.

Efan took a deep breath. A fresh, green smell filled his lungs and pulled him across the street. Above and around him were the dark, crowded trees. Under him was a quiet carpet of needles. Efan felt close and warm. Like someone was hugging him. His body felt light and dizzy. He was sure that if he lifted both his feet off the ground, he would float straight upward. Like an angel, he thought. A Christmas angel.

"Hey, little brother, need some help?" The voice creaked like a broken door. A tiny old man with skin like

dead brown leaves stood beside him. He was wearing a warm wool vest and a funny hat.

Efan straightened his shoulders and tried to look important. "Let's see now," he said, rubbing his chin real slow like a grown-up. "I want to buy a Christmas tree. A pretty one like that." He pointed to a medium-sized tree that was standing all by itself in the center of the lot, looking as if it owned the place. "How much?" Efan asked, taking out his money.

"Twenty dollars," the man creaked.

"Twenty dollars! Who has twenty dollars to spend for a Christmas tree?"

"Some people does." The man looked around the lot at all the people buying trees. "And some people doesn't," he said, looking at Efan. "But maybe I can swing you a deal." He took out a pad and a pencil and started figuring.

Efan closed his eyes and smiled. He could see his mother, Mean Margaret, and Old Woman standing in front of the beautiful tree, hugging him, on Christmas morning.

"Fifteen dollars, how's that?"

Efan looked down at the green-needled ground. "Thanks, Mister, but I ain't got that kind of money either." He turned his back on the man and started to walk away.

In the corner, leaning against the brick wall of the Emporium, was a tiny tree no bigger than a bush. It was thin and ugly, and it didn't even reach Efan's chin.

"Hey, Mister, how much for that runt over there?"

"Twelve. Ten dollars is as low as I can go."

Efan stuffed his savings into his pocket and dragged the tree back to the wall. Some plan! he thought, leaning against an old gray car. Looks like there'll be no Christmas after all.

Then Efan saw the woman. She was carrying a tree. Suddenly Efan was running up to her.

"Need some help, Lady?" The words popped from his mouth faster than buttons off an old coat.

"Thanks. My car's over there." She pointed to the old gray car Efan had been leaning against. "Could you put it in the trunk?" she asked.

"Sure." Efan lifted the heavy tree and positioned it under his arm. It was full and round and just the right size for his living room. He walked slowly toward the car, looking down at his feet. His left sneaker went out and took a step, and then his right sneaker went out and took a step. His left, then his right. Efan thought how easy it would be to run away with the tree. Left foot. Right foot. Left foot. Right foot. Before he knew it, he could be running down the street. Running as fast as he could go. Feeling the weight of the tree, but running just the same. Away from the lot. Toward 128th Street. Quick as he could. Home.

"You gonna load my tree, or what?" the woman asked.

Efan came out of his dream. He was standing by the lady's car. Not moving. Feeling terrible.

"Sure," Efan answered quietly. He put the tree into the trunk of the lady's car.

"Thanks," she said, pressing something cold and hard into his hand.

Efan looked down. There, on a quarter, was George Washington, wearing his ponytail and not smiling.

Efan still didn't have enough money to buy a tree. He felt even sadder than before. All he knew was he'd never

had a tree. All he knew was how much he wanted one.

"Hey, what's your name?" a creaky voice asked. "Mine's Jimmy."

It was the old man who owned the lot.

"Efan. Efan Little."

"Okay, Little Efan. Seems like you need a Christmas tree real bad. How'd you like to work for one? At the end of the night, whichever tree's left belongs to you. Deal?"

"Oh, Mister! Jimmy! It's a deal!" Efan reached out his hand, and Jimmy grinned and slapped it.

For the rest of the morning, Efan cut rope and un-furled the beautiful arms of the Christmas trees. It was hard work. The rope was thick, and the branches were heavy. "Ouch," Efan yelled. "You're pretty, but you're mean. Now I know why they call you needles instead of leaves. Feels like I've been to the doctor."

One tree was especially mean. It stuck Efan so hard, his fingers started to bleed. But when he finally cut the last bit of rope and opened the branches, he knew why the tree had put up such a fight. It was small and delicate, like a girl wearing a long green skirt. "You're something else," Efan said, breathing its deep perfume. "You're perfect. And just the right size. I'm gonna bring you home tonight and take special care of you. You won't be sorry."

Gently he lifted the tree and brought it to the back of the lot where no one would see it. Then he went back to work, feeling happy and humming his Christmas song.

Around one o'clock, just when Efan had untied the last of the trees, Jimmy came up to him and handed him a cup of steaming chili and a thick slice of bread. "From the store," he said.

They sat on one of the cars, watching the people in the lot and eating lunch. Efan told Jimmy about his mother and Mean Margaret and Old Woman, and how they didn't have a Christmas tree. And Jimmy told Efan how every year, a few weeks before Christmas, the Christmas tree trucks rolled in from way up North, where there was nothing but miles and miles of quiet and only the trees, the mountains, and the sky.

Efan closed his eyes and tried to imagine a place with no noise, no people, and no sidewalks or buildings. A place where the air smelled fresh and clean and green all the time. No wonder those trees tried to stick you. They must be plenty mad to have to leave a place like that.

"Have you ever seen it?" he asked Jimmy.

"What?"

"The place where the trees live."

"Nope. But one day, when I save up enough money, I'm gonna go. To the country. Away from all this cement. It's another world up there."

"Like heaven," Efan said. "With no gates."

All afternoon, Efan worked in the lot, selling trees.

"I've got the perfect one for you. Tall. Pretty. Look just right in your living room."

"I've got the perfect one for you. Small. Round. Look just right by your sofa."

By dinner time, almost all the trees had been sold. Efan and Jimmy sat on a car, eating ham sandwiches and drinking cocoa. It was dark out. The city was softer now.

Quieter. Like someone had spread a huge blanket over it.

A few people were still looking for trees. From way in the back of the lot, one of them called out. Jimmy climbed down from the car. An old man was waving some money and dragging Efan's tree. Efan sat still. He couldn't move. He could barely breathe.

"This little one was hiding in the back." The man laughed slowly. "Must have known I was coming for it. Gonna make my grandchildren mighty happy." He handed Jimmy the money, put the tree under his arm, and disappeared into the night.

"Jimmy!" Efan cried out. "That was my tree. I was saving it for Mama and Mean Margaret and Old Woman and me. Jimmy!" Suddenly Efan was crying. Jimmy held him in his arms and mumbled something over and over. Efan was crying so loudly, he couldn't hear what Jimmy was saying. But then he quieted down and heard Jimmy's words.

"There, there, little one. There, there. I'm sorry. I'm really sorry."

When Efan's body stopped shaking, he raised his head and looked at Jimmy. Jimmy's eyes were wet. Two small dark puddles.

"Let's choose you another one and mark it reserved. NO ONE ALLOWED TO HAVE THIS TREE EXCEPT EFAN." He took Efan by the hand and walked him through the lot. "You're in luck, Efan Little. Only the tallest trees are left." He grabbed a twelve-footer. "How 'bout this one? Looks to me like it's got your name on it."

Efan shook his head sadly. "Maybe a giant's name. But not mine. It won't fit in our house. No way. It's too big. They're all too big."

For a long time, Jimmy didn't say anything. He just

stared at his feet. Then, soft as a cat rubbing someone's leg, he whispered, "Sorry, Efan."

Jimmy looked so sad. Efan took his hand. "I'll get someone to saw it. Caboose! He lives on my street. He'll do it."

It was a lie. Caboose didn't own a saw. But even so, Efan felt better. It was a good idea. Surely someone on 128th Street had a saw. And anyway, all of a sudden, Efan was smiling and so was Jimmy.

"You're something, Efan Little. You're something." Jimmy's teeth flashed white against his brown face. "Let's load you up with this giant and get you home. Sky is turning funny-colored. Looks like we're in for a storm."

Jimmy and Efan tied up the branches of the big tree and attached a long piece of rope for Efan to pull.

"See you around," Efan said, trying to sound real casual, as if he didn't feel like crying.

"So long, Efan Little. Hope you have a real good Christmas," Jimmy said, and hugged him.

Efan dragged the tree through the streets. It was so heavy, he could hardly tell if he was pulling the tree or if it was pulling him. A cold wind blew off the river and tried to knock Efan down.

"Now I know how horses feel," Efan said, as he crossed 125th Street. "You're much too heavy and big. Gonna find a saw and cut you down to size."

Efan thought of all the people on 128th Street who might have a saw. Old Woman, Mrs. Gadsden, Caboose, the High Tones, Spider Stokes. Not one of them had a

saw. And not one of them, not even Spider Stokes, had a tree.

But then Efan had an idea. The best idea he'd ever had. It was such a good idea that it made the tree feel light as air. It even made Efan feel light as air. Efan started to dance. The tree bounced up and down behind him, and he sang his Christmas song.

"Hmmm muh muh
Do wah wah dee
I'm gonna get us
A Christmas tree."

When Efan finally reached 128th Street, the street was deserted. Everyone was in for the night. Mean Margaret must be madder than a wild dog, wondering where he was. And Mama must be back from the supermarket, worrying herself sick. But Efan wasn't ready to go home yet. He had work to do.

He dragged the big tree to the end of the street, near the cement wall of the highway. He rolled some of the trash barrels to the side and cleared a space. He emptied one of the barrels and filled it with rocks and old bottles. Then he untied the tree and spread out the branches. With all his strength, he lifted the heavy tree and stuck it in the barrel.

"My, you're pretty. Pretty as that tree down where Mr. Rockefeller lives."

The wind took a deep breath and blew real hard, and the tree nodded at Efan.

"You know you're pretty, but you'll be even prettier when I get finished."

Efan took a small carton out of the trash. All around him on the ground were pieces of broken glass. Green and clear glass from soda bottles. Brown glass from beer bottles. Even some red glass from an old car light. Very carefully, Efan put the glass into his box. Then he collected metal rings from soda cans. Some he twisted. Some he linked together. He put the lid on one of the trash barrels and climbed on top of it. One by one he hung the rings on the tree and laid the glass on the thick branches.

On the ground, he found a small piece of black crayon, and on the back of a piece of cardboard, he wrote:

Merry Christmas to 128th Street!
Signed,
The Bringer of Christmas,
Efan the Great

He stuck the cardboard under the tree and looked up at his work. The moon peeked out from behind a thick gray cloud and smiled down at him. The rings and glass sparkled.

"Don't have a star for you to wear on your head," Efan said. "But you're a queen anyway. The Queen of 128th Street."

The wind blew again, the tree bowed to Efan, and Efan bowed to it. "Don't go anywhere," Efan said, and he turned and went home.

26

That night, Efan dreamed that he and Jimmy were beating drums and leading a parade of marching Christmas trees. When Efan opened his eyes, he could still hear the drums beating. He reached his arms over his head and stretched the sleep from his body. Then he remembered. He was awake, and it was Christmas Day. But the drums were still beating. In fact, they were beating outside his window and at his door.

"Efan Little, get yourself out here." Old Woman was pounding at his window. "It's a true Christmas miracle."

Then Mean Margaret stopped knocking at his door and burst into his room. Behind her was his mother, smiling and shining like the sun. Margaret danced up and down on her toes.

"How'd you do it, Efan? Tell us, Efan. How?" she asked.

"Yes, Efan. Tell us," his mother said.

"Oh, Mama, I wanted to buy us Christmas, but I couldn't—so I made it instead!"

His mother shook her head and looked confused. She hugged him tight. "Well, you sure are making a lot of people happy this day. Get on your clothes. We're going out. The whole street is outside!"

In three minutes, Efan was dressed and at the door to his building. When he opened it, and went outside, he saw that Old Woman was right. It really was a true Christmas miracle.

It had snowed during the night, and the world, like a beautiful cake, was covered with icing. From the end of the street, Efan heard singing. It was the High Tones. They were standing under the tree singing Christmas carols. Even Spider Stokes was out. He was pacing up and down

in front of the tree, guarding it. Caboose was cleaning away some of the trash. Old Woman was whistling and standing on a stepladder, decorating the tree with chains of popcorn and bird seed. Mrs. Gadsden was dancing in the street. All around, people were laughing and playing and building snowmen and snowwomen. The sun watched over the tree and turned the metal rings to silver, and the glass to diamonds and emeralds and rubies and gold. And at the very top, where there should have been a star, one of Old Woman's birds sat coughing and cooing at everyone below.

Efan's mother hugged him. Even Mean Margaret hugged him. The air was thick and sweet with Christmas. Efan could smell it and taste it.

"Efan Little! Efan Little!" the buildings and the street seemed to shout. "You brought Christmas. You brought Christmas to 128th Street."

"I know." Efan smiled and nodded. "I know."

Merry Christmas to 128th
Street.

signed,
The Bringer of Christmas
Efan the Great